The Tale of Tom Kitten

A Story about Good Behavior

Retold by Judith Adams
Illustrated by Nina Barbaresi

Famous Fables

Reader's Digest Young Families

Once there were three little kittens, and their names were Moppet, Mittens, and Tom Kitten. The kittens loved to play outside. By the end of the day, their soft, furry coats were usually very dirty!

One day the kittens' mother, Mrs. Tabitha Twitchit, invited her friends for tea. She wanted the children to look especially neat for her company. So she called the kittens inside to wash them and brush them and comb them.

Mrs. Tabitha Twitchit dipped a sponge in water and scrubbed each kitten's face.

Next, the kittens' mother gently brushed their fur.
Then, she carefully combed the kittens' tails and
whiskers. Tom Kitten did not like to be combed. He
was naughty and almost scratched his mother's paw.

Mrs. Tabitha Twitchit dressed Mittens and Moppet in lacy white dresses. Then she went to a drawer and pulled out a fancy blue jacket and blue pants for Tom Kitten to wear.

When the kittens were all dressed, their mother sent them out into the garden to be out of her way while she prepared treats for her visitors.

"Now keep your clothes clean, children!" said their mother.

"Let's climb up the rocks and sit on the garden wall," said Moppet. Mittens thought that was a good idea.

They skipped and jumped their way up the rocks. Moppet's kerchief fell off and landed in the dirt.

Tom Kitten couldn't jump very well in the pants he was wearing. Instead, he had to climb up the rocks very slowly. And as he climbed, all but one of his buttons popped off. They flew in every direction!

By the time Tom Kitten reached the top of the wall, he was a mess. Moppet and Mittens tried to straighten his jacket and pants, but things didn't get better. First, Tom's hat fell off. Then, his last button popped off.

While the kittens were having so much trouble, they heard something strange. *Pit pat paddle pat! Pit pat paddle pat!* Then they saw the three Puddle-ducks coming down the road. One duck led and the other two followed. They stopped in front of the kittens and stared up at them.

The Puddle-ducks were named Rebecca, Jemima, and Drake. Rebecca picked up Moppet's kerchief and put it on. Jemima Puddle-duck picked up Tom's hat and put it on.

Moppet laughed. She laughed so hard that she fell off the wall. Mittens and Tom Kitten climbed down after her. By the time the kittens reached the ground, they had lost the rest of their clothes.

Moppet stepped up to Drake Puddle-duck, who liked to be called Mr. Drake. "Please help us put Tom's clothes back on," she said, "and let's make sure they don't fall off again!"

Mr. Drake listened to Moppet. He moved sideways toward the clothes and picked up each piece with his beak. Then he dressed *himself* in Tom Kitten's clothing!

The suit fit Mr. Drake even worse than it fit Tom Kitten. Mr. Drake didn't seem to mind. Jemima and Rebecca Puddle-duck put on the two dresses. The three Puddle-ducks marched up the road walking their funny walk. *Pit pat paddle pat! Pit pat paddle pat!*

When Mrs. Tabitha Twitchit went out to the garden, she couldn't believe her eyes! The kittens were sitting there without any of their clothes. She put them on the path to the house. Then she scolded them and shooed them inside.

"My friends will be here any minute and you are a mess," said Mrs. Tabitha Twitchit. "I am not happy with you—not happy at all." She sent the kittens to their room.

When her friends arrived, they heard loud thumps and crashes coming from upstairs. They couldn't imagine what could be making such strange noises.

Mittens, Moppet, and Tom Kitten were having a wonderful time, tumbling and playing, as kittens will do.

Meanwhile, the Puddle-ducks waded into a pond wearing the kittens' clothes. The clothing fell right off and sank to the bottom of the pond.

Mr. Drake, Rebecca, and Jemima Puddle-duck have been looking for the lost clothes ever since. That is why they keep dipping their heads into the water, as ducks will do.

Famous Fables, Lasting Virtues

Tips for Parents

Now that you've read The Tale of Tom Kitten, *use these pages as a guide in teaching your child the virtues in the story. By talking about the story and its message and engaging in the suggested activities, you can help your child develop good judgment and a strong moral character.*

About Good Behavior

Part of growing up for young children is learning to distinguish between what is right and what is wrong. Children also must learn to change their behavior in a positive way. For parents, the challenge is not only teaching the difference between right and wrong but also instilling in their children the desire to act responsibly. Here are a few helpful strategies:

1. *Show your child that you respect her.* Increase your level of praise when your child behaves well. Listen to your child, even when she misbehaves. This shows you value what she has to say. When appropriate, let your child make choices. This shows you trust her to make good decisions for herself.

2. *Resist the impulse to step in and act on behalf of your child when things don't go as planned.* Children learn through doing, experiencing, and even failing. While it's important for parents to show love and offer guidance, let your child try to solve her own problems when you feel it is appropriate.

3. *Set clear expectations and stick to them.* Rather than assume your child knows what is right and wrong, sit down together and draw up a list of family rules for all family members to follow.

4. *Impose natural consequences whenever possible.* If your child refuses to dress for school, put her clothes in a bag and take her to school in her pajamas. If she insists on wearing a party dress to the playground, don't offer to buy her a new one if it gets torn or dirty.